45p

Beanstalk Books

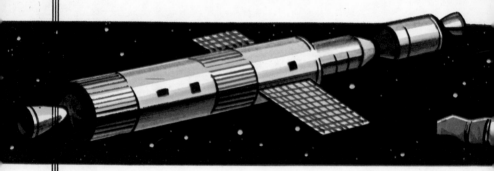

Reading Consultant: Dr Elizabeth Goodacre
© 1974 Thomas Nelson & Sons Limited
SBN: 72380992 5
Printed in Great Britain by W. S. Cowell, Ipswich

SPACE EMERGENCY

Written by

Alan Blackwood

Illustrated by

Philip Corke

NELSON
YOUNG WORLD

"What a picture, what a great picture!" cried Captain Mark Fox.

He was taking pictures of the sun inside Space Station 9. The space station was in orbit hundreds of miles above the Earth.

"You could never see the sun like this back on Earth," he said. "You need to be out in space, with no air, to see the sun, the planets and the stars so clearly."

"Right Mark," agreed his friend Commander Peter Hanson. "And take a look at this!"

From another window of the space station they could see the Moon. It was far clearer and brighter than when seen from Earth.

"Beautiful!" said Captain Fox. "I can see the place where the first Moon landing was made, back in 1969."

Commander Hanson looked at his watch. "Time to contact Earth Control," he said.

Commander Hanson switched on his receiver.

"Hallo Earth Control. Space Station 9 reporting. Over."

There was no reply. Commander Hanson repeated his signal. There was still no reply. He adjusted the receiver. There was a lot of crackling, but nothing from Earth Control.

"Something's wrong," he said.

Commander Hanson thought for a moment.

"It might just be very bad interference from solar flares," he said. "But my guess is that the radio antennae on the outside of the space station have been damaged. Maybe we've been hit by a small meteorite. That could have done it. Think I'd better go out and take a look."

13

Captain Fox helped Commander Hanson into his space suit.

Inside the space station there was air and warmth. The astronauts could breathe easily. They could wear comfortable overalls. But outside the space station there was nothing, just empty space and immense cold. A man could not live in space without a space suit to give him oxygen and keep him warm.

Commander Hanson fitted his helmet in place and checked that his oxygen supply was working properly. Then he climbed into the space station air lock. He closed the inside door of the air lock behind him. He opened the outside door and pushed himself out into space.

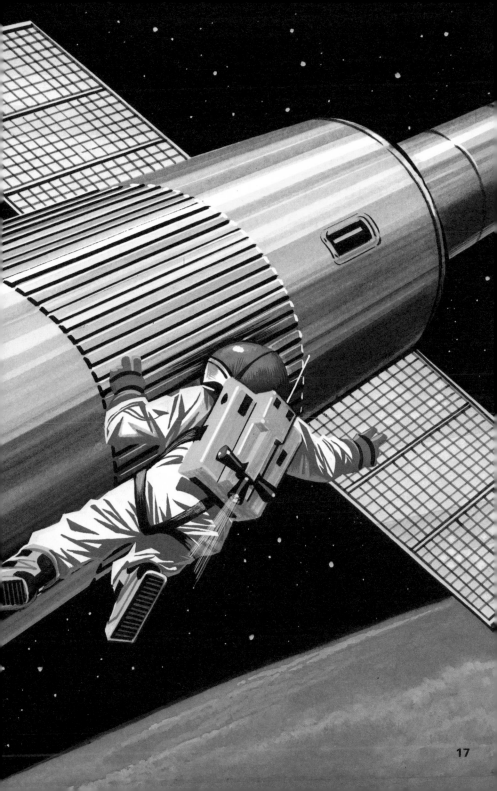

Fox saw Hanson switch on his "space gun", which he used to propel himself through space. Hanson's voice came over the intercom.

"I've found the trouble, Mark. It was the radio antennae, just as I thought. Shouldn't take long to fix. Think I'll inspect the rest of the space station while I'm out here."

Fox saw Hanson move past a window. Then, suddenly, he saw the jet from his space gun die out.

"Hallo Mark," Hanson called urgently over the intercom. "My space gun's failed. I'm drifting."

"I know Pete," Fox replied. "I saw it happen. I'll be out there as fast as I can."

This was a real emergency. When the space gun failed it had been propelling Hanson away from the side of the space station. With nothing to slow him down, he would keep drifting away from the space station, unless Fox could get to him.

Fox worked as fast as he could to get into his own space suit. It was a difficult job without help.

But at last he had his oxygen pack strapped to his back, and his helmet firmly in place. Then he too stepped into the air lock, and into the starry blackness of space.

He held his breath as he switched on his own space gun. Thank goodness it worked.

"I'm on my way, Pete," he called over the intercom.

By the time the two astronauts met up, the space station seemed a very long way off.

"Do you think we'll make it back to the space station?" Fox asked.

"We'd better, Mark," Hanson replied. "You don't want to be a dead spaceman floating on through eternity, do you?"

When at last they got back inside the space station Earth Control were calling them.

Commander Hanson reported back and explained what had happened.

"You men sure had an emergency," said the man at Earth Control. "Now you'd better find out what's wrong with that space gun. Take it to bits. Let us know the trouble."

Hanson and Fox grinned at each other. Back to work!